AR
26704

2.7

At the Police Station

This book is dedicated to Major R. Small.

Grateful Acknowledgment is made to
the City of Chicago Police Department

Design and Art Direction
Lindaanne Donohoe Design

Picture Acknowledgement
©Phil Martin—Cover, 14, 16, 18, 24
Courtesy of the City of Chicago PoliceDepartment:
Steve Herbert—3, 4, 6, 8, 10, 12, 20, 22, 24, 26, 28, 30

At the Police Station

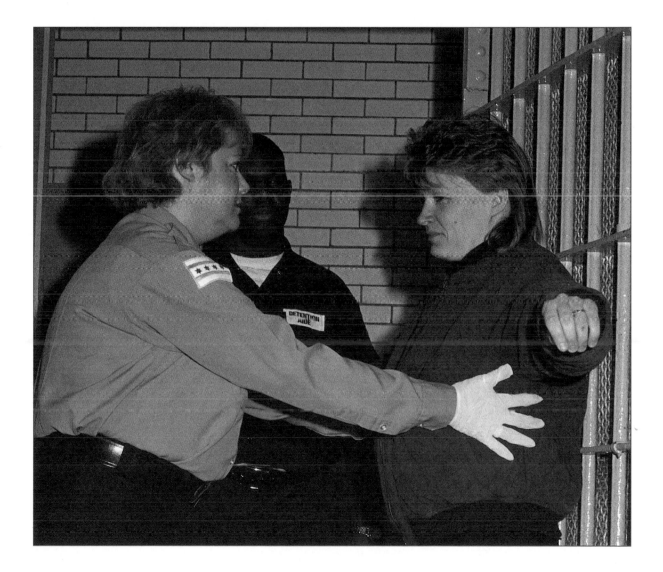

By Carol Greene

The Child's World®

It's morning at the police station.
A group of officers comes on duty.
Police officers work eight hours a day.
This is called a shift.

There are
three shifts each day.
The police station
never closes.

In the squad room, the officers learn what
has happened since their last shift.
They find out which car they will drive and
which part of town they will protect.

Some officers
work in pairs.
Some work alone.

Sometimes officers watch training videos
in the squad room.
Other times they take special classes there.

Police officers must keep up with a lot of information.

In the dispatch area, officers answer phone calls. They type information from the calls into a computer. Then they radio the information to a patrol car.

Some patrol cars have computer terminals in them. The dispatcher can send information right to them.

BRRRING!

It's a 911 emergency call.

At once a special screen shows the address
and phone number of the caller.

WHIRRR!

This big tape machine records all calls
to the police station.

911 is an important phone number. If you need help in a hurry, call 911 and the police will come.

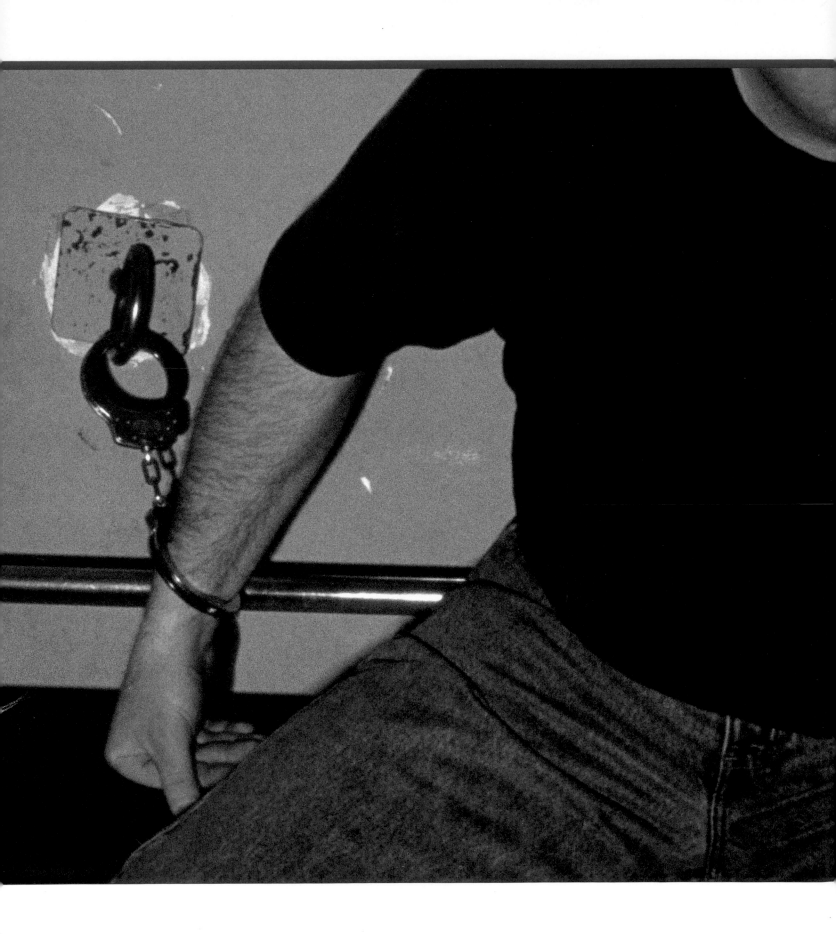

These officers caught a man trying to break into a house. First they take him to the booking room in the police station.

If the man is fighting, the officers may handcuff him.

M F

Right Thumb

TENPRINTER

They take his fingerprints.

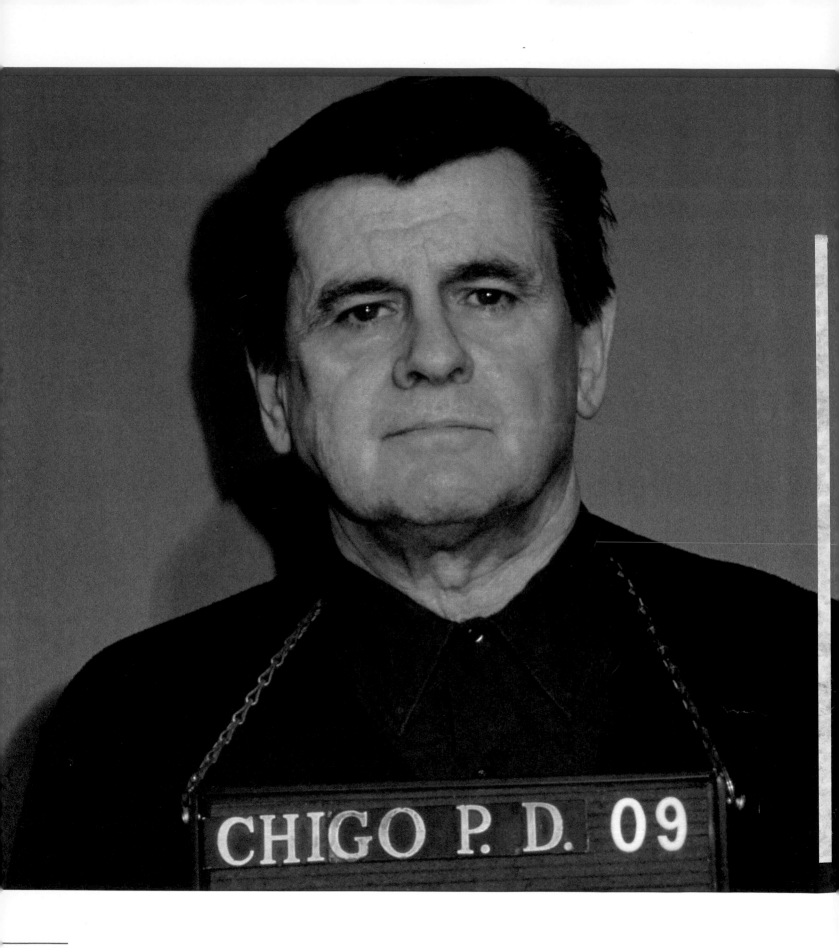

FLASH!!!

They take his picture too.

CLANG!

The officers put the man in a holdover cell.

He will stay there until all the paperwork is done.

Then he will be moved to the city or county jail.

A holdover cell is not a nice place to be.

Cameras watch everything that happens in the holdover cells. The pictures are shown on screens. A police officer is always watching.

It's no fun being watched all the time.

The police check their files in the records room.
They check their computer records too.
It will tell the officers if the man has committed
a crime anywhere else in the country.

This machine works by computer.

It can tell if a person has had too much to drink.

Police officers use this machine to check out drunk drivers.

Don't drink and drive!

The shift is almost over.
Some officers write reports about
what they've done.

Some police officers put their reports on computers.

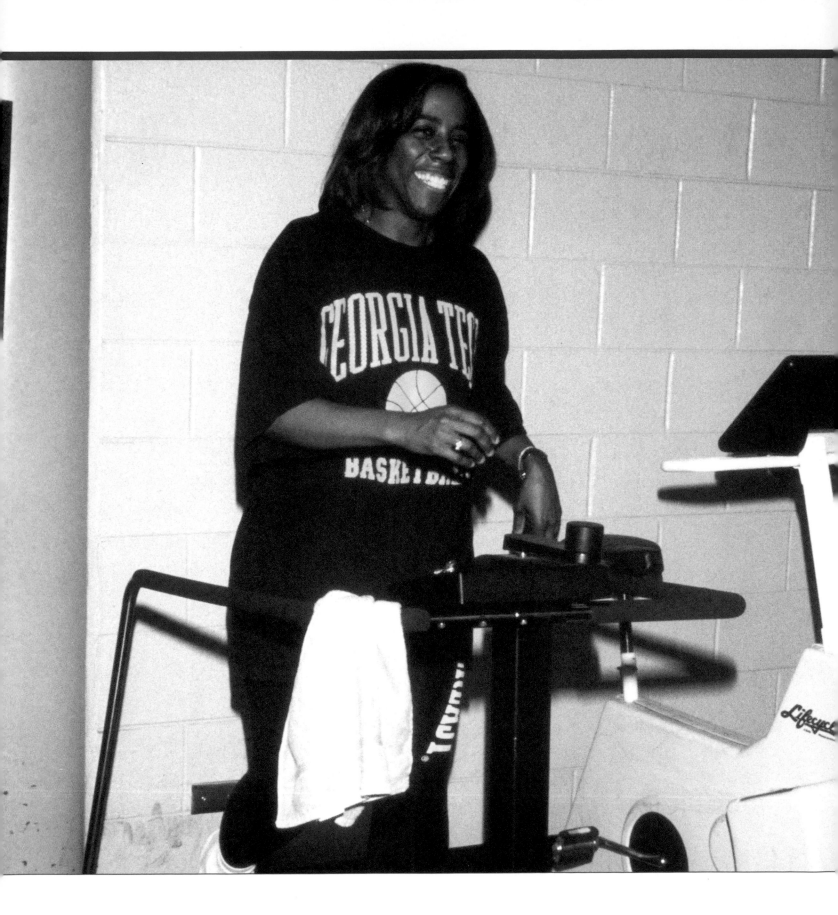

This officer decided to work out in the exercise room.
But everyone else goes home.

Glossary

booking room—the room in a police station where suspects are questioned

dispatch—to send out messages or people

computer terminal (kom PYOO tuhr TER min uhl)—the keyboard and visual display of a computer

holdover cell—the place where prisoners are held for a short time

records room—the room in a police station where the paper and computer files are kept

shifts—a change from one group of officers to another

squad room (SKWAHD ROOM)—the room in a police station where officers meet

About the Author

Carol Greene has written over 200 books for children. She also likes to read books, make teddy bears, work in her garden, and sing. Ms. Greene lives in Webster Grover, Missouri.